D0387022

Aug 20

A TRIP to the COUNTRY for MARVIN & JAMES

The Masterpiece Adventures **BOOK FIVE**

A TRIP to the COUNTRY

for MARVIN & JAMES

ELISE BROACH

Illustrated by

KELLY MURPHY

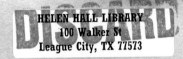

Christy Ottaviano Books

Henry Holt and Company • NEW YORK

Henry Holt and Company, *Publishers since 1866*
Henry Holt® is a registered trademark of Macmillan Publishing Group, LLC
120 Broadway, New York, NY 10271
mackids.com

Library of Congress Cataloging-in-Publication Data is available.
ISBN 978-1-250-18609-6

Our books may be purchased in bulk for promotional, educational, or business use. Please
contact your local bookseller or the Macmillan Corporate and Premium Sales Department at
(800) 221-7945 ext. 5442 or by email at MacmillanSpecialMarkets@macmillan.com.

First edition, 2020 / Designed by April Ward and Sophie Erb

The artist used pen and ink on Coventry Rag paper to create the illustrations for this book.
Printed in the United States of America by LSC Communications, Harrisonburg, Virginia

1   3   5   7   9   10   8   6   4   2

For my friend Jill Lepore, who
loves the country as much as I do

—E. B.

For my friend Jasper,
who is full of great stories

—K. M.

Contents

CHAPTER ONE

Riding the Train

Marvin and Elaine cannot believe how lucky they are. They are going on a trip with James! James's father, Karl, and his wife, Christina, have a house in the country, and James is going to see it for the first time. He will have a *sleepover*.

So many new things at once! It's very exciting.

Yesterday, James asked Marvin, "Do you want to come? Would you like to bring your friend?" Of course Marvin did want to go, and of course his cousin, Elaine, wanted to go too. To their great surprise, Mama, Papa, Uncle Albert, and Aunt Edith said yes.

Nobody in Marvin's family has ever been to the country. They've lived in the city all their lives. But they have heard wonderful stories about the country from other beetles, like the ladybugs that sometimes visit the Pompadays' apartment. The country has fields of grass and corn and strawberries. There is so much to see, and do, and *eat*. Marvin and Elaine can hardly wait.

So today, here they are, hurrying through the train station with Mrs. Pompaday. Marvin and Elaine are in James's shirt pocket, peeking out.

"Marvin, this place is huge!" Elaine cries. "I have never been anywhere this big in my entire life. And there are so many people." She grabs one of Marvin's legs. "Be careful you don't fall out or you will be smashed flat as a pancake."

"I won't," Marvin says, annoyed.

Elaine always thinks about bad things that can happen, especially bad things that can happen to Marvin.

Mrs. Pompaday stops suddenly. "James, here's your train," she says, pointing to a sign.

They go through a tall, dark doorway, and straight ahead of them is the train. It is long and silver.

"Let's find you a good seat," Mrs.
Pompaday says. "You must be very
careful, James. Don't talk to strangers.
Just sit and look out the window, and
when the conductor comes, give him
this." She holds out a little piece of
paper. "This is your ticket. Don't lose it!
Let's put it in your shirt pocket."

Wait, what?! Marvin and Elaine duck down. What if Mrs. Pompaday sees them?

"That's okay, Mom," James says quickly. He grabs the ticket just as Mrs. Pompaday is tucking it in his pocket, poking Marvin and Elaine. "I'll put it in my pants pocket."

Phew!

Marvin and Elaine are too afraid
to climb back to the top of the shirt
pocket, so they can only hear bits of
what Mrs. Pompaday is saying. She
is talking a lot. They hear her say,
"Hold on to your ticket . . . Karl and
Christina will be waiting for you . . .
It's the eighth stop."

Finally, they see James's eyes, big above them. "Are you okay, little guy?" he whispers. "Is your friend okay?"

Marvin and Elaine crawl to the top of the pocket.

"That was close!" James says. He smiles. "Look, I'm on the train. All by myself. Well, except for you guys."

Marvin looks around. James is sitting by the window, with his backpack next to him, and now the train is starting to move. It bumps and rumbles through the darkness.

"Why is it so dark outside?" Elaine asks.

"We must be underground," Marvin says. "In a tunnel below the city." Beetles know all about tunnels. They make tunnels inside walls and beneath floors.

"Do you think it will be like this all the way to the country?" Elaine asks. She sounds disappointed.

Marvin hopes not . . . even though beetles can see well at night, much better than humans. In the tunnel, he notices pipes and cables along the train tracks.

"Look! There's a rat," Elaine cries.
And Marvin sees it too, a big rat
sniffing some garbage on a nearby track.

Elaine shivers. "Oh Marvin, thank
goodness we're inside this train.
Remember Aunt Lulu?"

How could Marvin forget poor Aunt
Lulu, who was collecting crumbs under
the Pompadays' kitchen table one night

when she was surprised by a mouse.

"Isn't it strange to think that we could be FOOD?" Elaine says. "Why, a rat could probably eat a whole family of beetles! I wonder what we taste like."

"Stop, Elaine," Marvin says. He is not enjoying this talk one bit. He is very glad when there's a burst of sunlight and the train roars outside.

Marvin sees sky and streets and tall buildings.

James sits up to look out the window. "Wow, cool!" he says.

And then something bad happens. As James kneels on the seat, the ticket in his pants pocket falls out!

It drops into the tiny space between the seat and the wall of the train, out of sight.

James does not notice. He is busy looking out the window.

"James lost his ticket!" Marvin tells Elaine. "It fell down there."

"Oh no!" Elaine says. "What if they make him get off the train?"

That would be terrible. They are still in the city, but far from home.

"Then we won't get to see the country," Elaine says sadly. Marvin thinks that is the least of their problems.

"Maybe I can get it," he tells her.

"Do you think you can? Be careful,
Marvin. There's not much room for
you. What if you get stuck?"

"I won't get stuck," Marvin says.

"You might. And what if you're
trapped there, riding this train forever?"

Marvin crawls out of the pocket
and down James's shirt.

"Well," Elaine calls to him, "don't worry. If something happens to you, I will be friends with James."

Marvin ignores her. He leaps onto the seat and slips into the tiny space between the seat and the wall.

Where's the ticket?

At first he doesn't see it. It is so thin . . .

Did it fall all the way to the floor?

No. There it is, pressed against the wall.

Marvin crawls to it and grabs it with his front legs.

He tugs.

He can move it, but it is heavier than he thought. The paper slips out of his grasp. He tries to drag it up to the seat cushion.

"I can't see you," Elaine calls. "Are you stuck?"

"No," Marvin says. "I've got the ticket, but I can't pull it up."

"Well, you'd better hurry," Elaine says. "I see a man coming and he's taking everyone's tickets."

Marvin hears a loud voice. "Tickets! Have your tickets ready, please."

And then James says, "Uh-oh. Where's my ticket?"

Marvin doesn't know what to do.

He tugs and tugs, but the ticket is stuck.

Then he has an idea. If he can't pull the ticket, maybe he can push it down to the floor.

With all his strength, Marvin pushes the ticket. It slides out and falls to the floor.

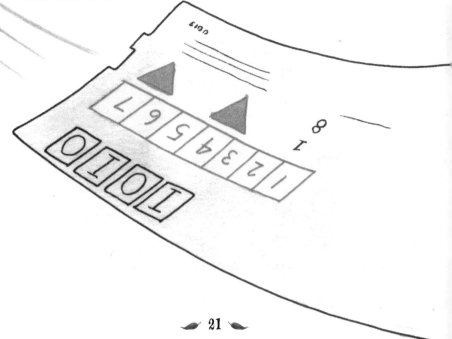

Marvin quickly crawls back up to the seat cushion. James is turning around in his seat, looking everywhere. For a minute, Marvin is afraid James might kneel on him by accident.

But then James sees Marvin.

"Little guy, what are you doing down there?" He picks Marvin up. "I lost my ticket! I must have dropped it."

Marvin races to the end of James's finger and dangles off the tip, waving his front legs at the floor.

"There it is!" James says with a rush of relief. "You found it."

The man taking tickets is standing next to James's seat. "Ticket, please," he says.

James quickly puts Marvin back in his shirt pocket.

"Here it is," he says, picking the ticket up off the floor.

The man takes the ticket and does something that makes a clicking noise. Then he gives it back to James.

"Look, he made a little hole in it," Elaine says.

"Be careful with your ticket," the man says. "You'll need it for the ride back."

"Okay," James says. When the man leaves, James whispers to Marvin, "Thanks, little guy. You were a big help."

It makes Marvin happy to help James. That's what friends are for. And Marvin has learned that even someone small can be a big help. In fact, being small can sometimes be the best way to help someone big.

"It's a good thing we found that ticket," Elaine says. "What would James have done without us?"

Marvin sighs. He settles into the pocket with Elaine as the train rumbles toward the country.

CHAPTER TWO
The Country House

They have been riding a long time. Outside the train window, the tall buildings are gone. The sky is wide and blue. There are lots of trees, and sometimes there's water. Is that a river? A lake? Marvin isn't sure.

"Oh, Marvin, look how pretty it is!" Elaine says. "Is this the country? Are we here?"

"I don't know," Marvin says. "But it doesn't look like the city."

Finally, James says, "Okay, it's the next stop." He sounds excited, and a little nervous. He grabs his backpack.

The train groans and rolls to a stop. James checks his pocket to make sure Marvin and Elaine are safe, then he gets up. When the doors of the train open, he steps off.

"James! James!" Karl and Christina are waiting there, just like Mrs. Pompaday said they would be.

They rush over and hug James.

"Let me carry that," Karl says, taking James's backpack. "Our car is right here."

"We're so happy you came! How was the ride?" Christina asks.

"It was fun," James says.

Marvin is not surprised that James doesn't tell them about the lost ticket. Grown-ups worry about that kind of thing, even when the trouble has passed.

They all get in the car and now they are riding on a road with trees and fields on either side. Marvin and Elaine can't stop looking out the window. They see a barn, and then a fence with sheep behind it. Marvin has never seen real sheep before.

"This is the country, Marvin!" Elaine says. "Did you know it would be like this?"

"No," Marvin says. He has seen pictures of the country in books James reads, and he has seen the country on TV. But here, in front of them, it is so big and green and full of new things. Already, Marvin is very happy they came. He can't wait for the ride to be over so he can crawl around and explore.

After a while, the car turns off the road, and Karl drives slowly over bumpy dirt. Up ahead, Marvin can see a white house. There are yellow and blue flowers growing by the porch.

"Look, buddy, we're here," Karl says. "Isn't it great?"

"Cool!" James says. He opens the window and leans his head out. Marvin feels the warm, fresh breeze. It smells sweet and grassy, nothing like the city.

The car stops.

"You must be tired of sitting, James," Christina says. "Why don't you have a look around while your dad and I make lunch?"

"Okay," James says. He opens the car door and races into the house.

Marvin and Elaine hold tight to the edge of his pocket. "I wish he would slow down," Elaine says. "I'm getting an upset stomach."

James runs around the house, opening doors, climbing the stairs. Marvin and Elaine bounce back and forth in his pocket. "Hey," he yells. "Is this my room? The green one?"

"Yes!" Karl calls. "It's all ready for you."

Marvin can see that the room is freshly painted. There's a bed with two puffy pillows, a desk with a lamp,

and a shelf with books and toys and
games on it. Marvin sees a little car,
a toy sailboat, and a tractor with
a wagon.

And then he sees something that
makes him happiest of all. On the desk
is a stack of paper, and a new pen-and-
ink set!

"Wow, Dad, you got me another ink
set!" James yells.

"I sure did," Karl calls up the stairs. "So you can draw when you come stay with us."

Marvin can't believe it. Whenever James comes to the country, he can draw pictures—which means Marvin can draw pictures too!

James gently takes Marvin and Elaine out of his pocket. "Look, you guys," he whispers. "This is my new bedroom. Let's make a sign for the door."

He sets Marvin and Elaine on the desk and opens the bottle of ink. "Here, little guy, you can help me," he says, putting the cap in front of Marvin.

Yay! The first thing Marvin will get to do in the country is draw a picture.

James uses the pen to write J–A–M–E–S across a sheet of paper. Marvin dips his front legs in the tiny pool of ink in the cap. What should he draw?

Something new.

A sheep!

Carefully, in the corner of the paper, Marvin draws the fluffy body of a sheep, and its four skinny legs.

"Oh, look!" Elaine cries. "That's the sheep we saw. Marvin, you are such a good drawer. You can draw anything."

James looks at the picture. "I like that," he says. "Maybe I'll draw a horse to go with it."

Karl and Christina appear in the bedroom doorway. Marvin and Elaine quickly duck behind the lamp.

"Time for lunch," Karl says.

"How do you like your room?"
Christina asks.

"I love it," James tells her.

"Oh, look at your great sign," Karl
says. "We'll get some tape and put it on
your door."

"Yeah," says James, "so everybody
knows this is my room."

He follows them downstairs to lunch.

Marvin and Elaine crawl out from behind the lamp.

"Drat," says Elaine. "I wanted to go outside and explore. Now James is going to forget about us."

"No, he won't," Marvin says.
"James never forgets about us. He'll
be back soon . . . and we can explore
in here while we wait."

Elaine sighs. "Okay, I guess. Let's
see what's on this shelf."

She crawls across the desk and onto
the bookcase next to it. Marvin follows
her.

"What's this?" she asks, pointing to something hard and round, with a long string coming out of it.

Marvin has never seen anything like it before. "I don't know," he says. "Maybe it's a toy?"

"What do you think it does?" Elaine asks.

The string dangles over the edge of the bookshelf.

"Let's swing on it," Elaine decides.

Marvin is afraid they might fall. "I don't know."

"Oh, come on. It will be fun." Elaine grabs the string and pulls it up to where they are standing. "Watch me," she says.

She holds on to the string and before Marvin can stop her, she jumps off the shelf.

"Wheeeeeeeee!" she cries.

She swings back and forth through the air.

"Marvin, I'm flying!"

Secretly, Marvin has always wished he could fly. Whenever he sees a flying bug—a gnat, or a moth, or a bee— he imagines how free he would feel, sailing through the air. The closest he has come to that feeling is the time he made a parachute out of a tissue, in the Pompadays' bathroom.

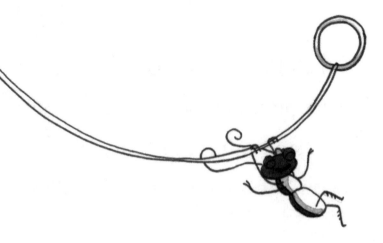

Elaine swings wildly through the air. "Marvin, you have to try it," she calls. "This is so much fun."

When the rope stops swinging, Marvin pulls her back up to the shelf. She hands him the string. "Now hold on tight, and jump," she orders.

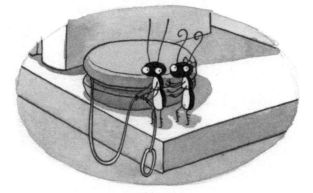

Marvin looks down. The floor is far below. "Are you sure that thing won't roll off the shelf?"

"Don't be silly," Elaine says. "It didn't when I jumped. You're barely bigger than I am."

"Well, make sure it doesn't fall on me," he says. He grabs the string and peers down.

"Do you want me to give you a little push?" Elaine asks.

"No!" Marvin says.

He takes a deep breath.

Then he jumps into the air.

Marvin is falling . . .

Falling . . .

Falling . . .

. . . and then the string snaps tight, and he is flying!

Back and forth, back and forth, he whizzes through the air.

"Look at me!" he shouts. "I'm flying!"

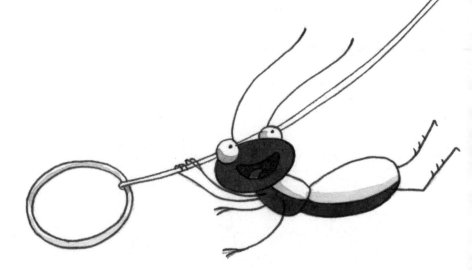

The books and toys on the bookcase blur past him as he swings.

"See?" Elaine yells. "Isn't it fun?"

It certainly is. Marvin loves flying.

When the string finally slows to a stop, Elaine pulls Marvin back up to the shelf. They take turns swinging until James comes into the room.

"Hey, you found the yo-yo," he says. "Are you hungry? Here's some lunch."

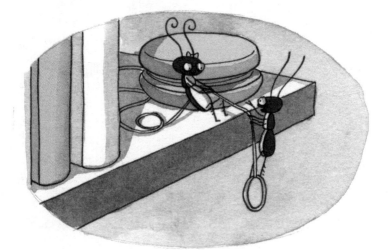

He unfolds a piece of paper towel on the desk. Inside are two blueberries, a potato chip, a corner crust of bread, and a little wet morsel of tuna fish. A feast!

Marvin and Elaine can't finish it, but they have a taste of everything. The blueberries are sweet. The potato chip is salty.

"Yum!" Elaine says as she takes a bite of tuna fish. "This will last us all weekend."

After their lunch, James tucks them in his shirt pocket. "There's a creek in the backyard," he tells them. "Let's take this boat and go play."

He picks up the little toy sailboat.

Marvin and Elaine cannot believe their luck. First they got to fly, now they will get to sail! There is so much to do in the country.

CHAPTER THREE
The Creek

Behind the house, across the field, is a brown creek. The water flows over rocks that shine in the sun. Trees grow along the muddy banks, and Marvin sees a dragonfly land on the tall grass.

James sees it too. "Wow, a dragonfly!"

The dragonfly is green and blue, with long silver wings. It darts through the air.

James kneels on the bank of the creek.

"First, let's see how fast the water is going," he says. He puts the sailboat in the creek.

They all watch. The boat floats gently down the creek until it bumps into a pair of rocks. James has to lean over the water to get it.

"Do you want to go for a ride?" he asks Marvin.

Of course Marvin does! He crawls onto James's finger, and James sets him down in the middle of the sailboat. It has a cabin with windows, benches in the back, two oars, and a beautiful white sail.

"What about your friend?" James
asks.

Elaine climbs out of the pocket,
stretching her legs toward James's
finger. He picks her up and puts her in
the boat.

"Ready?" he asks. "Anchors away!"

The little boat rocks and dips, floating down the creek. Marvin and Elaine are sailing!

"Oh my goodness, what a fancy boat," Elaine says. "Marvin, it's like we're on a cruise!"

They look over the sides at the brown water rippling past. They can see pebbles on the bottom of the creek, and sometimes a tiny fish. On the banks of the creek, there are waving grasses and patches of flowers.

"This is great!" Marvin says. He and Elaine sit on the benches in the back of the boat as it drifts downstream.

They see James waiting for them up ahead. He puts his hand in the water and catches the boat, carefully picking them up.

"Did you like that?" he asks. "Want to go again?"

Of course they do! They float down the creek again and again. Each time, they see something new: a mossy rock, a stick poking out of the mud, little black tadpoles swimming. Up ahead, a long wooden board lies across the water.

James says, "I know! You can go under the bridge."

He is just leaning over to set the sailboat in the water when a big yellow dog comes splashing into the creek.

"Hey!" James shouts, laughing. He drops the boat. *Plop!*

Suddenly, Marvin and Elaine are spinning downstream.

"Oooo, we're going fast!" Elaine says.

"Hold on," Marvin tells her, gripping the side of the boat. Water sprays his face.

"I'm coming," James calls, but they can see he's playing with the dog. The dog is jumping and wagging its tail, licking him.

The sailboat floats toward the bridge.

"Watch out!" Marvin yells. He and Elaine grab the sides of the boat as it sails under the dark board.

Then they are out in the sunlight again, floating down the creek. There are more rocks here. The boat bumps into a big one and shifts back and forth, almost turning over.

"Ooomph," Elaine says, holding her stomach. "This is making me seasick."

"Me too," Marvin says. "Where's James?"

They know he isn't far away, but they're ready to get out of the boat. Elaine grabs one of the little oars and tries to steer toward the muddy bank.

Finally, the boat comes to rest in a patch of tall grass.

"Good," Elaine says. "Now we can relax."

They are just stretching out in the sun when Marvin gets a strange feeling.

It is the feeling of being watched.

There in the reeds is a big, spotted frog.

"A frog!" Marvin shouts.

The frog's long, sticky tongue comes straight toward him, fast as a whip.

Elaine leaps up and smacks the frog's tongue with the oar.

It sucks the oar back into its mouth. *Snap!*

"Quick," Marvin cries. He snatches Elaine's leg and pulls her over the side of the boat.

"But Marvin, I can't swim—"

They tumble into the water just as the hungry frog tries again to eat them.

CHAPTER FOUR
Sink or Swim

The cold water rushes over Marvin and Elaine. Marvin is an excellent swimmer, but he has never gone swimming in a creek before. The water is moving so fast, and Elaine, who can't swim at all, is trying to climb on top of Marvin's head.

They are sinking below the surface, gasping for air.

"Elaine," Marvin yells. "You're pushing me under. You have to hold on to my back."

"But I'll drown!" Elaine cries. "I need to be up high."

She crawls on top of Marvin's head again and now Marvin nearly drowns.

Finally, he gets Elaine to wrap her front legs over his shoulders. Now he can swim.

Marvin tries to paddle toward the bank but the water is going too fast. His legs quickly get tired.

"There's a big rock," Elaine says, pointing. "Swim that way."

Marvin thinks it must be nice to ride on someone else's back and give orders. As best he can, he swims toward the rock.

It is slippery with moss, but Elaine finds a spot where she can get a grip. She climbs off Marvin's back. Then she helps him up.

They try to catch their breath.

"Marvin, you nearly died!" Elaine says. "Thank goodness I saved you. That mean frog would have gobbled you up. Why, you would be sitting inside its belly right now if I hadn't—"

"Elaine," Marvin says, "stop."

Elaine frowns. "I'm just saying, you're lucky I was there."

Marvin is not feeling very lucky. They are stuck on a rock in the middle of the creek, and James doesn't know where they are.

They can see James walking along the bank. The dog is gone. James is holding the empty sailboat and calling, "Little guy! Where are you?"

What are they going to do now?

"I hate to say it, Marvin," Elaine

says. "But you may have to swim to the

shore. James will never find us on this

rock."

Marvin does not like this idea. "The

water is going too fast! I won't make it."

"Well, what are we going to do? We can't stay here," Elaine says.

They are stumped. The rock is dark and wet. Even if James looks this way, he won't see their black shells.

Then Marvin spots the dragonfly hovering over the tall grasses.

"Let's see if she can help us," he says.

Marvin and Elaine start waving their legs and yelling to the dragonfly. "Hey! Over here!"

"What's the matter?" the dragonfly calls. "Are you stuck?"

"Yes! Can you go get that boy?" Marvin shouts. "If you fly near him, he'll see you. Then you can land over here by us, and he'll know where we are."

The dragonfly does not look happy. "That sounds like a lot of work," she says.

"Please!" Elaine cries. She points at Marvin. "He nearly got eaten by a frog! I had to save him."

"Oh brother," Marvin mutters.

But the dragonfly knows about frogs. "You poor thing," she says. "I had a close call with that frog myself. Okay, I'll help. But are you sure the boy won't try to catch me?"

"He won't," Marvin promises. "He's kind to insects."

"Okay, here goes," says the dragonfly.

She zips along the bank toward James.

He is bent over the creek, poking in the grasses with a long stick. She darts in front of his face.

"Oh!" he cries. The dragonfly makes shimmering circles in the air.

"Look at her," says Elaine. "Show-off."

But the dragonfly gets James to watch her. She flies straight to the rock where Marvin and Elaine are waiting and lands next to them.

James walks along the creek, dragging his stick. He still doesn't see Marvin and Elaine.

"Honestly," the dragonfly says. "Humans are so slow."

She flutters up again and flies in front of James's face. Then she darts back to the rock and hovers over Marvin and Elaine with her big silver wings shining in the sun.

"There you are!" James shouts, smiling. "I was afraid I lost you!"

Phew!

Marvin waves his thanks to the dragonfly.

She soars away, calling, "Glad to be of service!"

James stretches his long stick across the water to the rock. "Can you climb on this and crawl to me?"

Elaine looks at the stick. "Do you think that's safe?" she asks Marvin.

"If James says it is," Marvin answers.

Carefully, he climbs on top of the stick.

Elaine follows.

They crawl over the bumpy bark.

The brown creek flows beneath them.

Finally they reach the end of the stick and climb into James's hands.

"Yes!" James says. "You made it!"

Marvin and Elaine breathe a sigh of relief as James tucks them safely back into his shirt pocket.

CHAPTER FIVE

City or Country, Friends Forever

After the excitement of the boat ride, Marvin and Elaine are ready for a rest. They ride in James's pocket as he walks across the field.

He comes to a long fence with a barn behind it. "This is where that yellow dog lives," he tells them. "I wish I could have a dog."

Elaine makes a face at Marvin. Marvin is not afraid of dogs, because dogs don't bother beetles. But Elaine does not like the way dogs drool and slobber.

James looks down at them. "Maybe my dad and Christina will let me have a dog out here in the country."

Elaine looks at Marvin. "I hope they don't! What if James likes dogs more than beetles?"

But Marvin isn't worried about that. If James wants a dog, Marvin hopes he will get one. James is his best friend, and when James is happy, Marvin is happy.

James takes them out of his pocket and puts them on the fence post.

"Look," cries Elaine. "Goats!"

On the other side of the fence, looking at them with interest, are five goats. One goat hops up on a stump.

"Aren't they funny?" James says. "And see, there's a horse too."

Over by the barn, a brown horse starts walking slowly toward them, ears pricked.

"Let's feed him some grass," James says. He picks a handful of grass and holds it over the fence. The horse comes closer.

"Look how big he is," Elaine whispers
to Marvin.

The horse rubs his soft nose against
James's hand and eats the grass. Soon
the goats come too, and even though
they are standing in a field full of grass,
they also want James to feed them.

Elaine and Marvin sit on the rail of the fence in the warm sun, watching the animals. "Isn't this nice, Marvin?" Elaine asks. "Don't you think it would be fun to live here?"

All around them is the country—the big fields, the rushing creek, fences and trees and wide blue sky. It's so different from the city. It is quiet. It is green. It is full of animals, not people.

"Yes!" says Marvin.

"Well," Elaine says quickly, "I would miss my mother and father. But maybe the next time James comes here to visit, our whole family could come— we could have a beetle vacation in the country!"

Marvin thinks that Mama and Papa would like that . . . eating the country food, seeing the sights, breathing the fresh, clean air.

"That's a great idea," Marvin tells Elaine. "Let's look for a place that would make a good beetle country house."

"Then we won't be city beetles anymore," Elaine says. "We'll be country beetles."

Country beetles! That would be something new.

"Do you think James will still like you if you're a country beetle?" Elaine asks.

"Of course he will," Marvin says. "No matter where we are, James and I will always be friends." He looks up at James. "James and I will be friends forever."

Marvin sees that the horse and the goats have gone back to eating the grass in their own pasture. James is resting his hand on the fence rail, so Marvin crawls on top of James's finger.

"Hi, little guy," James says. "Let's go back to the house. You and your friend can finish your lunch."

Marvin has to admit he is hungry again after their adventure in the creek.

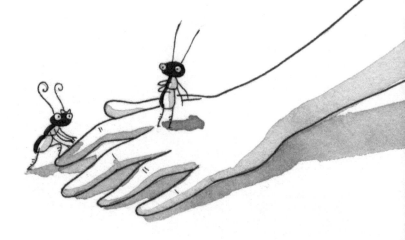

James picks up Elaine and puts them both in his pocket. Together, they cross the field.

Marvin can see Karl and Christina on the back steps. "James," they call. "Do you want to go blueberry picking?"

"Sure!" James yells.

"We almost went last weekend," Christina says, "but we thought it would be more fun to do it with you."

Marvin and Elaine bob gently in James's pocket as he walks toward the house, the sun warm on their faces.

"Do you really think you and James will stay friends?" Elaine asks. "What about when you grow up? And James grows up?"

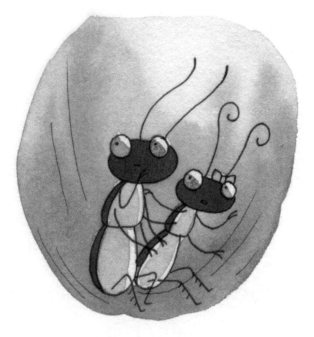

Marvin thinks about this.

"We'll still be the same inside," he says.

He looks up at James. He and James have done so many things together. They've made pictures, had adventures, helped each other, and cheered each other up.

Of course they'll stay friends. Marvin is sure. No matter where they go, no matter how big or old or grown-up they become . . . inside their hearts, a boy and his beetle will always be friends.